Mr. Mango
Follow Your Heart

Written by Annie Serravalle

Character Designs by
Victoria Buddle

Story Illustrations by
Cedge Productions

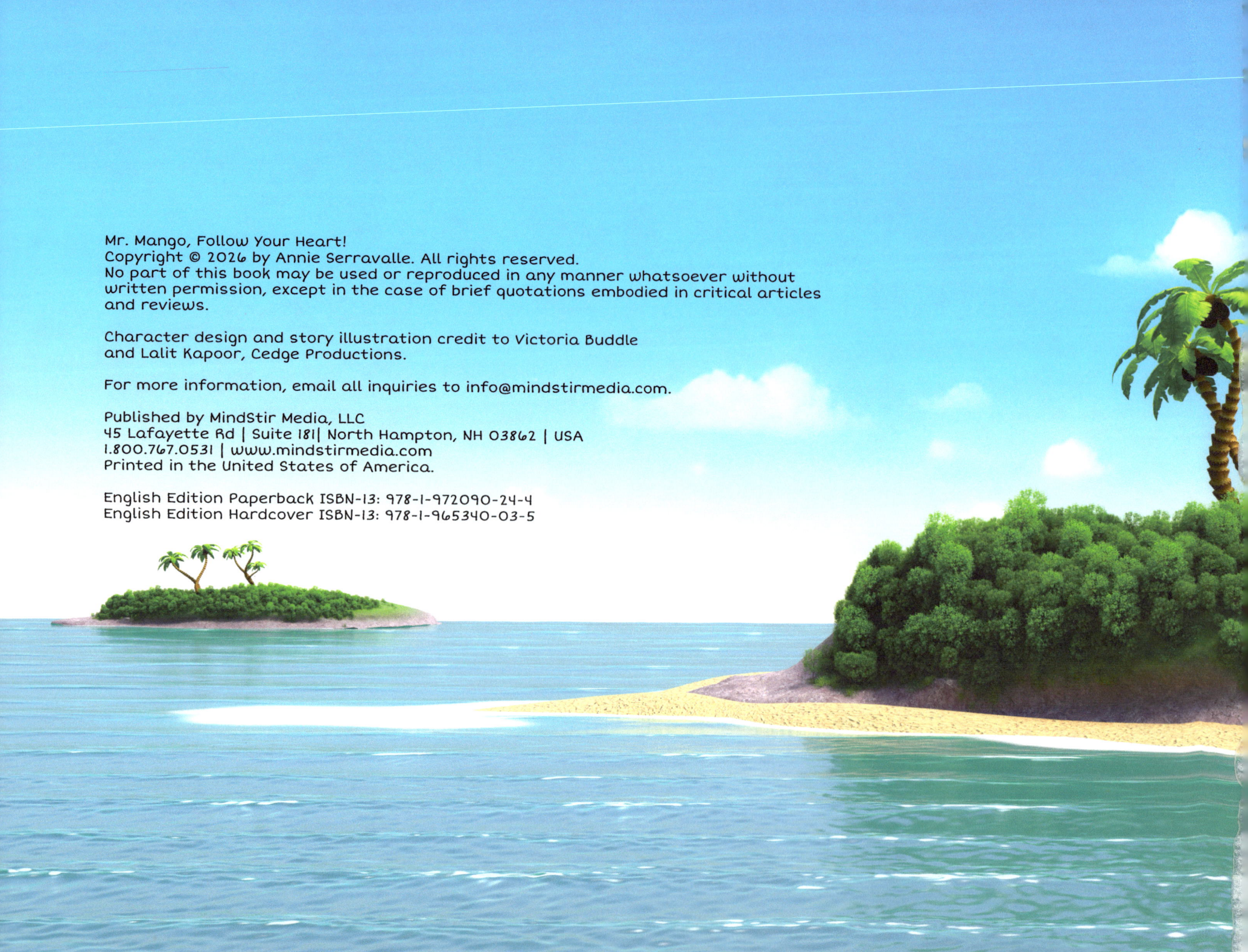

Character design and story illustration credit to Victoria Buddle
and Lalit Kapoor, Cedge Productions.

For more information, email all inquiries to info@mindstirmedia.com.

Published by MindStir Media, LLC
45 Lafayette Rd | Suite 181| North Hampton, NH 03862 | USA
1.800.767.0531 | www.mindstirmedia.com
Printed in the United States of America.

English Edition Paperback ISBN-13: 978-1-972090-24-4
English Edition Hardcover ISBN-13: 978-1-965340-03-5

A brief note ♪ from
Annie to Mr. Mango's team...

I would like to dedicate my premiere book,
Mr. Mango Follow Your Heart, to the Mr. Mango Productions team!

I want to thank my exceptional project editor and dear friend, Gail,
and my fantastic book editors, Madison, Alyssa, and Jackie.

I am grateful for the support from Naveen, Victoria, Lalit,
Kostadin, Marco, Jessena, Steve, Baileys, Cole, Monica, and Tom.
Your contributions mean everything to me.

To my family, thank you for your support.

Most of all, to my dear grandson Max,
who loves to read books. I hope this book,
Mr. Mango Follow Your Heart, finds a
special place in your heart, Max.
With all my love, Gramma

Carl the Coconut Tree

Wally the Wave

African Drumming Group

Skye the Sun

Sammy's Snack Stand

Sharpy the Shark

Anywhere

Mr. Mango's Hut

Yoga Lessons

Mr. Mango walks along the beach, feeling unhappy.

No one will dance with him, but he hopes to find a partner.

Mr. Mango will introduce you
to his friends at the beach.

Will he follow his heart?
Let's join him to see what happens next.

Mr. Mango lets out a big yawn as he stretches his arms above his head, gets out of bed, and slides into his flip-flops.

He walks towards
his dresser and
gazes at his
reflection in
the mirror.

Mr. Mango says, "Good morning, flower box friends! Do you think I will find my dance partner today?"

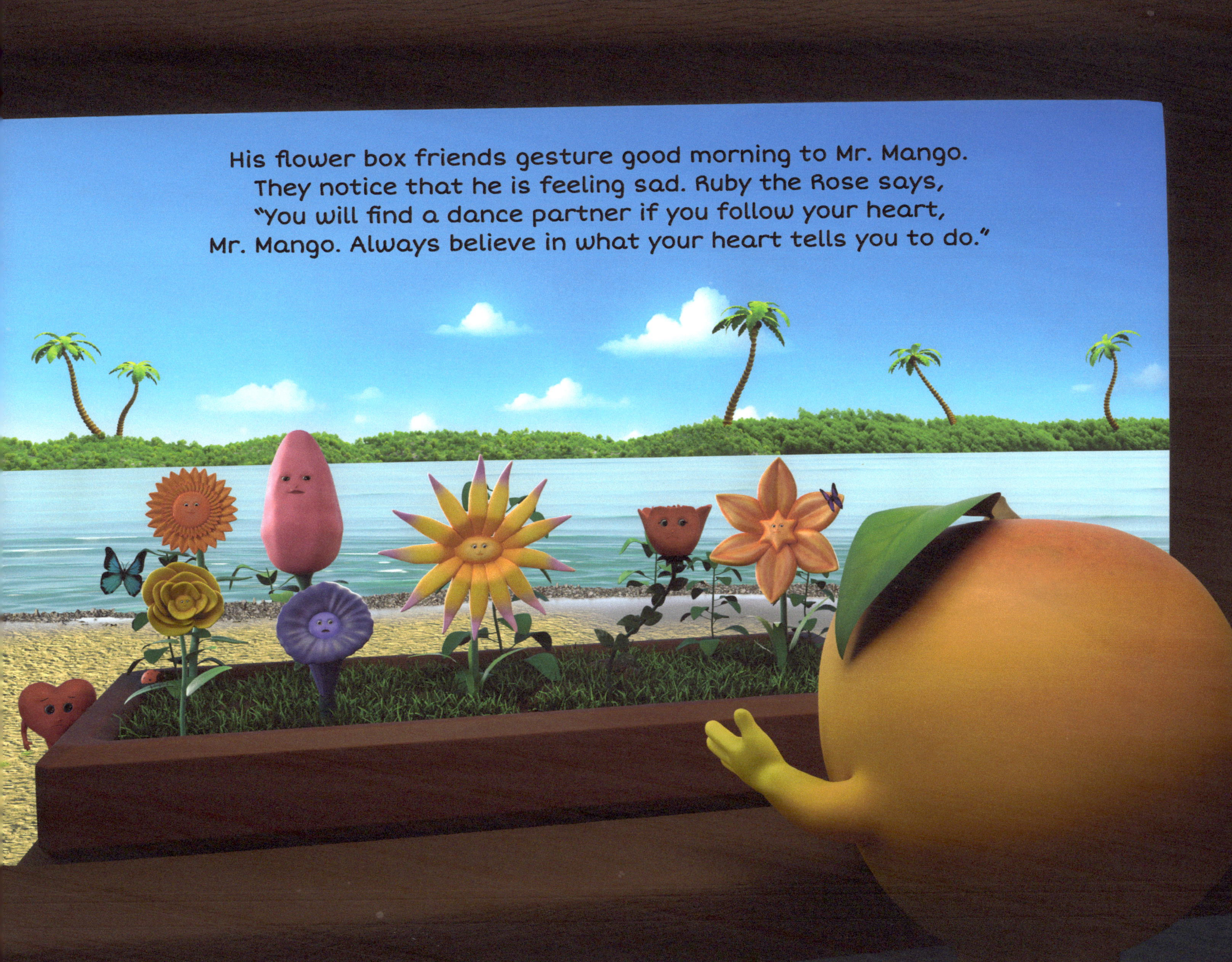

His flower box friends gesture good morning to Mr. Mango.
They notice that he is feeling sad. Ruby the Rose says,
"You will find a dance partner if you follow your heart,
Mr. Mango. Always believe in what your heart tells you to do."

Mr. Mango leaves his beach hut, walks down the stairs, and strolls along the beach in search of a dance partner. At the first stop on his journey, he decides to visit his best friend.

Carl the Coconut Tree greets Mr. Mango. "Are you still searching for a dance partner, my friend? I think you should follow your heart."

Mr. Mango replies, "I will find my dance partner someday, Carl. I just need to keep trying."

After visiting Carl, Mr. Mango
is greeted by Stanley the Sand Face.

Stanley says, "Hi, Mr. Mango! Why do you look so sad?
Are you still searching for that dance partner?
Well, look at me. I'll make you laugh!"

As the wind rises, Stanley spins faster, creating a sand funnel in the sky. Stanley disappears, leaving Mr. Mango covered in sand.

Mr. Mango exclaims,
"Stanley, that was magical!
Where are you? I can't see you."
Stanley replies,
"I can hear you. Just follow
your heart, and you will find your
dance partner."

Wally the Wave approaches the shore to comfort Mr. Mango after Stanley couldn't make him laugh. Wally says, "Could you please cheer up? I've noticed that you search for your dance partner here every day."

Wally the Wave and the smiling fish try to
cheer up Mr. Mango.
"Don't worry," says Wally. "You will find your
dance partner. Just follow your heart."

Mr. Mango and Wally are joined by Sharpy the Shark, who arrives on his new surfboard. Sharpy is such a show-off! Mr. Mango calls out, "Be careful, Sharpy."

Sharpy replies, "I'll be fine. Now follow your heart and go find your dance partner."

Mr. Mango sees four seashells basking in the sun: Susie, Sydney, Sara, and Sally.

They were the beach's biggest gossipers, and they were all laughing at him.

Susie asks,
"What brings you back to the beach today?
Are you still looking for a dance partner? You may never
find one. Just give up already. None of us wants to dance
with you. Please, just go away!"

Mr. Mango feels heartbroken.
He is so troubled and believes his heart
is no longer guiding him.

Talking to himself, he mutters,
"This is hopeless. I am hopeless. I'll never find anyone to dance with me."
Mr. Mango feels extremely upset.

He looks up at the sky
and falls onto the sand.

Waving his arms and legs
back and forth in the sand,
Mr. Mango creates a sand angel.
He feels quite sorry for himself.

As the sand angel rises from the golden sand, she gazes at Mr. Mango.
He asks his sand angel, "Who are you?"
She answers, "I am Sienna the Sand Angel, created by you, Mr. Mango.
You are kind to everyone. I am here to support you on your journey.
Believe in yourself and follow your heart."

Sienna draws three
hearts in the sky.
She says,
"I will watch over you
to ensure you follow your
heart, follow your heart,
follow your heart."

Sienna ascends into the sky, promising to watch over Mr. Mango as he continues his search. Mr. Mango whispers to himself, "I must follow my heart to find my dance partner."

As Mr. Mango continues his journey,
he notices that a beautiful sandcastle
ahead seems to be missing a flag on top.

As he approaches the sandcastle,
Mr. Mango discovers a seaweed flag
in the sand. He picks up the flag...

...He tosses the flag, landing it right on top of the sandcastle!

"Hooray!" the children shout. "It landed perfectly. You are so thoughtful, Mr. Mango, for helping us finish our sandcastle! Now, you run along and find your dance partner. Remember to follow your heart."

Mr. Mango calls back, "Wait! How did you know that?" The children reply, "Everyone knows you are looking for your dance partner."

Suddenly, the wind pushes against Mr. Mango's back.
He listens to the soothing voice of Sienna the Sand Angel,
coming from the clouds above.

She softly says, "Mr. Mango, follow your heart,
follow your heart, follow your heart. Keep moving forward.
Go find your dance partner."

Up ahead, Mr. Mango picks up the cheerful sound of rhythmic drumming coming from the beach. He pauses for a moment and gently sways back and forth, sensing the lively energy surrounding him...

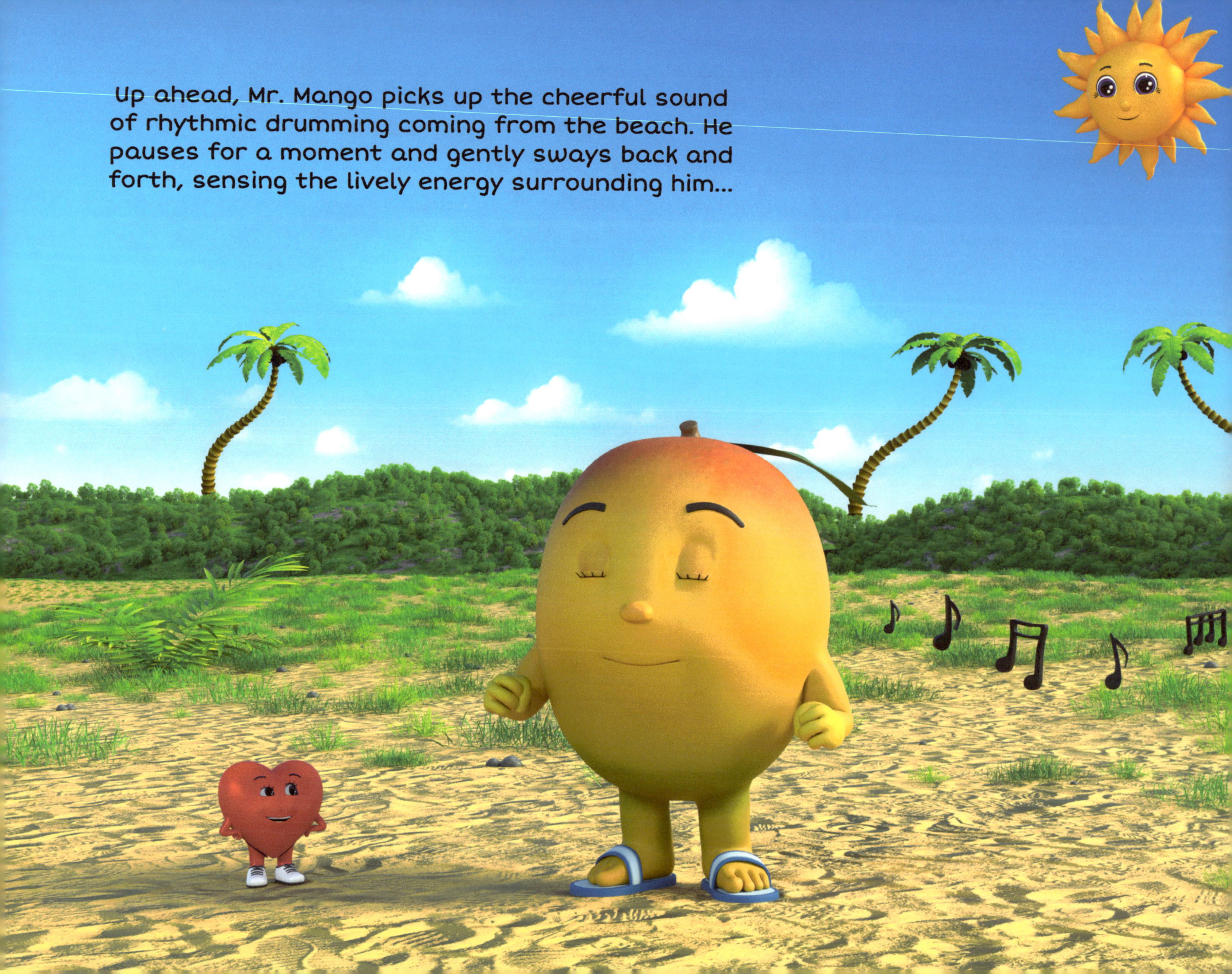

...from the vibrant beat
of the drums.

Dolly the Drummer exclaims, "Hello, Mr. Mango!
My name is Dolly. This is my African drumming group.
We love sharing our music with everyone on the beach
as they soak in the warmth from Skye the Sun."

"Well, hello to you, too, Dolly," Mr Mango replies.
Mr. Mango tells Dolly, "I'm searching for a dance
partner. My friends say I should follow my heart,
but I haven't found anyone to dance with yet."
Dolly believes she can help him.

Dolly joyfully extends her hand and invites
Mr. Mango to dance with her, making his heart
skip a beat. He can't help but whisper,
"This must be a dream!"

Skye the Sun sings a lovely melody for Mr. Mango and Dolly, casting warmth and light around them.

In this touching moment, Mr. Mango and Dolly the Drummer begin dancing the tango together!

Dolly's drummers create a perfect rhythm that musically complements the melody sung by Skye the Sun.

This is truly a beautiful moment. Mr. Mango and Dolly happily dancing together, their hearts filled with delight. Mr. Mango can hardly believe that he finally has such an excellent dance partner by his side. He wishes this moment could last forever!

Dolly the Drummer cheers for Mr. Mango, saying,
"You're a fantastic dancer! You followed your heart
and finally found your dance partner, and it's me!
You can dance with me anytime!"
"Thank you so much, Dolly," Mr. Mango replies.
"I will always remember your kindness."
As he says goodbye, he thinks, "At last! I can't
believe I've finally discovered my dance partner.
Hip hip hooray! I am so happy!"

Skye the Sun beams with joy for Mr. Mango. He gratefully thanks her for her lovely singing while dancing with Dolly. With a warm smile, she gently reminds him that it's nearly time to head back to his cozy hut before nightfall.

Sammy the Hot Dog Vendor and Hector the Hot Dog notice Mr. Mango returning to his beach hut wearing a big smile. They ask him, "Did you enjoy your day?"

Mr. Mango answers, "I'm so happy, Sammy! I finally followed my heart and found my dance partner. It's been a wonderful day! However, I'm pretty thirsty. May I have a soda?"

Sammy replies, "I am so happy for you, and of course, you may have a soda."

As soon as Mr. Mango requests
a soda, Sassy the Soda Can and the
playful ice cubes, Millie, Lilly, and Bonnie
pop out of the cooler.

ICEY COLD SODA

Sassy the Soda Can jumps
into Mr. Mango's left hand.

Then, Sassy the Soda Can jumps into Mr. Mango's right hand.

When Sassy lands
back on the hot dog stand,
Mr. Mango and his friends laugh
as she opens her can, spraying soda
everywhere! What a mess! It's wonderful
to see Mr. Mango smiling again!

Upon arriving at his beach hut,
Mr. Mango spots Yolanda, the yoga instructor.
Three seagulls rest nearby, breathing in the salty air
coming from everywhere. With a peaceful heart,
Mr. Mango joins his hands and says,
"Namaste!"

As he walks toward his beach hut,
Mr. Mango whistles a cheerful, sweet melody.

Dancing up the stairs,
Mr. Mango's heart swells with joy.

Mr. Mango happily returns to his cozy beach hut,
smiling as he reflects on the wonderful dance he shared with Dolly,
his delightful new dance partner. His cheerful flower box friends
greet him warmly, excited to see that he has finally
followed his heart.

As he waves goodnight to his flower box friends,
Mr. Mango closes his window shutters and prepares for bed.

Mr. Mango
takes off his flip-flops,
leaps onto his bed, and
snuggles under the
cozy blanket.

Lying in bed, Mr. Mango gazes at the beautiful reflection in the dresser mirror as the evening twilight filters through the window. He catches a glimpse of Dolly the Drummer waving goodnight.

Drifting off to sleep,
Mr. Mango reflects on
his dance with Dolly.
His heart whispers,
"Mr. Mango, I have always been by
your side. All you had to do was
follow me, and you did-

The Moral of this Story:

"Happiness can be found anywhere
if you just simply follow your heart."

Annie Serravalle / Author / Composer

Annie's musical journey began at the young age of seven when she took her first piano lesson. Over the years, her passion for music has blossomed into a rewarding career as a professional musician and a devoted music educator at her alma mater, an elementary school in Central Connecticut. Annie's enthusiasm for music education deepened, inspired by her outstanding music students and their challenges. She has embarked on an exciting new adventure as a children's book author, aiming to connect meaningfully with young audiences through her captivating stories, original songs, and vibrant animations featuring the delightful main character, Mr. Mango. By closely observing her students, Annie has discovered the unique hurdles children face, believing that these challenges can lead to positive outcomes. Through heartwarming tales of Mr. Mango, she offers children with joyful and uplifting lessons on how every problem can become a positive solution while cultivating essential social and emotional learning skills to support each child in developing a fulfilling life. This special connection with her students has inspired Annie to create her first children's story, compose and orchestrate an original children's song, and develop a magical animation titled "Mr. Mango Follow Your Heart."

Mr. Mango

Mr. Mango was born from Annie Serravalle's heart! His favorite colors are yellow, orange, green, and blue. He loves singing and dancing and adores all his storybook friends. Mr. Mango is very emotional and silly as he grooms the leaf on his head with Mango Mousse to make it shine! If his leaf is down, he feels sad; if it's high, he is very happy. If it's halfway up or down, he feels content. Most importantly, Mr. Mango loves helping children understand that conflicts in their lives always have resolutions. He assures them of this. He knows how to comfort children through his stories.

Character Designs and Story Illustrations

Victoria Buddle

From a young age, Victoria has loved art, starting with her first box of colored pencils. Her creative passion and artistic talent flourished as she drew and enjoyed Saturday morning cartoons with her grandfather. Now an elementary school art teacher in Connecticut, Victoria inspires her students with her enthusiasm for art. Although she never intended to be a children's book illustrator, Victoria believed in herself and turned her dream into a reality.

Tajinder Pal Singh, Arun Kashyap, Lalit Kapoor

Our team at CEDGE Productions is excited to combine our experience and creativity to enhance the beautiful illustrations by Victoria Buddle for "Mr. Mango Follow Your Heart." With the power of modern technology, we have transformed her captivating 2D drawings into dynamic 3D images that are sure to inspire and engage readers of this delightful storybook. This collaboration merges Victoria's original artistry with our enhancements, inviting readers to embark on a vibrant and uplifting visual journey.

Hey Everybody!

Feel free to scan the QR codes below, and don't hesitate to ask an adult for help if needed! Visit our website to discover all the amazing things Mr. Mango Productions has in store for you!

Mr. Mango Productions Website

Listen to our original song, "Mr. Mango Follow Your Heart"

At Mr. Mango Productions, we're truly passionate about creating delightful original children's storybooks that emphasize the importance of social and emotional learning! Our books come alive with charming original songs, captivating animations, and exciting choreographed dances for kids to enjoy. We're dedicated to nurturing emotionally confident children who will thrive beautifully in today's world.

Thank you for reading my premiere book, *Mr. Mango Follow Your Heart.*
I can't wait to share my upcoming adventures with you!

Goodnight, world.

www.ingramcontent.com/pod-product-compliance
Lightning Source LLC
Chambersburg PA
CBHW042218030726

47382CB00046B/188